Grandpa, Is Everything Black Bad?

Story by Sandy Lynne Holman

Illustrated by Lela Kometiani

For our Grandparents: Rufus, Willie Lee and Tamara

**Sandy gratefully acknowledges her family members, friends and colleagues
whose kind contributions helped to make this book possible...**

The Bettencourt Family
Jessica Brown
Lee Lipton & Scott Brown
Pedro & Doris Cordova
Aunt Barbara
Andria Fletcher
Marilyn Hays
Arline Holman

Roosevelt Holman
Toni Holman
Sharon King
Lela Kometiani
Russ & Carolyn Kusama
Pat McDaniel
Mark Miller

Samantha Kate Mueller
Toni Satchel
Jim & Sue Saum
Corwin Shropshire
Dorothy Starks
James & Ernestine Turner
Aunt Dorothy & Uncle Fred
Pam Wittpen

Summary: An illustrated story of an African American boy who comes to appreciate his dark skin by learning about his African heritage from his grandfather.
Publisher's Cataloging in Publication Data
√ **J 158.1-HOL**
ISBN: 0-9644655-0-7
LCCN: 95-067793

Grandpa,
Is Everything
Black Bad?

It's dark, **black** and scary
in my bedroom at night.
So I hide under the covers
when Dad turns out the light.

I like watching TV,
but sometimes I'm sad
because most white things are good
and most **black** things are bad.

People wear the color **black**
when somebody dies.
They look very sad
and have tears in their eyes.

Grandpa, is everything **black** bad?

Grandma says hide in a bush
when a **black** cat walks by
because they bring bad luck
to those that they eye.

Aunt Barbara says my skin
is darker than most others.
She calls me the **black** sheep of the family
because I look different from my brothers.

I saw a fire burning
in the forest one day.
It made the trees turn **black**
and the animals run away.

Grandpa, is everything **black** bad?

I think witches are scary
flying their brooms in crooked hats.
They always look ugly and
they always wear **black**.

I like hitting baseballs
with my friends, Ronnie and Tye.
One day our ball hit Jasmine's face
and she got a **black** eye.

Black widow spiders
are dangerous and quick.
They have poison in their bites
that can make people sick.

"Tell me Grandpa, is everything **black** bad? I'm black. So, does that make me bad too?"

"Hmmm. I reckon I can understand the way you feel, Montsho. Grandpy never did stop to think about all the things in this world that are the color black that seem bad. Maybe that's why so many chil'en are ashamed of their beautiful dark skin. You younguns think all dark things must be no good."

"So, it's true, huh, Grandpa? Everything black is bad," Montsho whispered sadly.

"Now, you wait jus' a minute little man. You ain't bad and neither is the color black. You jus' get that kinda thinkin' out of your head. It's folks who decide what colors mean to them. Why, I love the color black and think it's one of the most beautiful colors in the world," Grandpa said firmly.

"You do, Grandpa?" Montsho asked, surprised.

"Yep! I do, little man. Almost as much as you love your Grandma's gumbo soup."

"You see, Montsho? It ain't the color of someone's skin that makes them good or bad. It's what's inside their heart that counts. The more love you give from your heart, the better you are as a person, no matter what people say or do. You understand?"

Montsho nodded.

"You also have something else inside you that is very important."

"I do?" Montsho asked, curiously.

"Yep, you do, little man. You have a *Heritage*; a very, very proud heritage."

"Heritage?" Montsho wondered, wrinkling his face. What's heritage mean Grandpa?"

"A heritage is our past. It's where we come from. It's the traditions and the things that are important to us and our family who lived long before us. Our heritage is African, Montsho."

"African!" Montsho said loudly. "I'm not African. I don't live in Africa."

"No, but our ancestors did live in Africa a long time ago, and the spirit of Africa is within us no matter where we live. Africa is also where a lot of important things happened that helped people all over the world. Even today, you and I still have African blood in our bodies. That's why we look like the black Africans who still live there."

"So, why does everyone call me black, then?" Why don't they call me African?"

"Hmmm... I don't know, Montsho. Black folks have been called so many different names over time that maybe people aren't sure what we should be called anymore. Some folks say we should be called one thing and some say we should be called another. All Grandpy knows is that us grown-up folk got to be careful what we let our younguns be called. Especially if it makes them feel bad."

"We also have to teach y'all about your heritage."

"What do you like people to call you Grandpa?"

"Why... that's simple, little man. They can start by calling me by the name my mama gave me when I was born... 'Rufus.'"

"I didn't know your name was Rufus," Montsho said tickled.

"That's because to you I'm just plain ole 'Grandpy.'"

"If someone calls you black, do you feel bad, Grandpa?"

"No, Montsho, I don't. You see, when I was a youngun jus' like you, my grandfather taught me about our African heritage and our history. He gave me a special bamboo drum and as he played it, it told me stories from our past. Those stories made me feel mighty proud of my African heritage and the dark color of my skin."

"Could you play the drum for me now Grandpa?" Montsho yelled excitedly. "Could you please?"

The old man looked into Montsho's big black eyes and smiled. He took Montsho by the hand into a special room in the back of the house. The room was beautiful, flowing with colors of black, gold, purple, red and green. Beautiful African scenes were painted on the walls and masks and pots were lying on the floor. It looked like an African kingdom with a straw hut inside. Within the hut was a large, red, bamboo drum. It looked magical. Montsho's Grandpa sat him on the floor and began to slowly beat the drum with his large, old hands.

"Close your eyes, little man," Grandpa whispered. "Feel the love you have in your heart as I play. Listen and you will see pictures in your head as the drum tells you a story about our heritage and history."

Montsho closed his eyes and listened as his Grandpa beat the drum. After some time, the drum beat sounded like voices to Montsho. *Boom, boom, boom...*

Boom, boom, boom... The drum began to talk...

Africa is beautiful and so are its native people
with their beautiful, dark black skin.
Her lands have great animals, like lions, giraffes and elephants.
Africa is where our ancestor's lives begin.

Africa's land is naturally rich,
with lots of diamonds and gold.
With deserts and rain forests throughout her regions
Africa is beautiful to behold.

Africans built the mighty pyramids
and used some of the earliest tools.
They developed writing, mathematics, astronomy and religion.
Even the Greeks came to study at their schools.

The Nile river, the longest in the world,
was home to the earliest farms.
There were Queens and Kings in African lands.
Africans made medicines to keep people from harm.
Africans made calendars a long time ago
that today would still be right.
They had clocks like the sun dial they used in the day
and the water clock they used at night.

Africans had writing the Greeks called "Hieroglyphics,"
which used pictures in place of words.
Africans were proud and made important contributions
that have helped people all over the world.

Be proud of your dark skin.
It represents a proud people
and black is truly a beautiful color.
It was passed down to you by Africans who lived before
and your heritage is like no other.

Mostly, be proud of the love in your heart
and all you have within.
It's the love that you share with people around you
that matters the most in the end.

The drum kept talking to Montsho.

Boom, boom, boom...
Be proud of your black skin and the love you have within and remember your heritage is African.
Be proud of your black skin and the love you have within and remember your heritage is African.
Be proud of your black skin and the love you have within and remember your heritage is African.

At last, the drum stopped beating. Montsho opened his eyes and gave his Grandpa a big, strong hug.

"That was beautiful, Grandpa!" Montsho cried. "I saw pictures in my head. I saw Africa. Please, can we play the drum again? I want to know more about our past and our African heritage. I want to hear the drum talk again."

Montsho's grandfather put his arm around the little boy and said gently, "That's enough for today, little man. Grandpy's old bones need to rest. Besides, it is very important for you to remember what you learned today."

"Don't worry Grandpa. I won't forget what the drum said, ever!" Montsho said proudly.

"Now, that's the kinda talkin' Grandpy likes to hear from his little man. Makes an old man like me feel real good."

"Grandpa, can I ask you something else?" Montsho asked softly.

"What's that Montsho?"

"Do white people have a heritage?"

"Yes, they do little man...all people do."

"Then what's their heritage?" asked Montsho.

"Well, it depends on where they come from in the world, little man. A lot of white people's ancestors in this country came from Europe. So, their heritage is European."

"What's European, Grandpa?"

"That is a whole other story that Grandpa will have to tell you some other day. Don't you worry yourself none, though. We'll have plenty of time to learn about your African heritage and all the others in this world. Let's learn a little more about your own heritage first, and then it will be easier to learn about all the others."

"Grandpa."

"Yes, little man."

"I love you! You always make me feel good."

"I love you too," Grandpa said, looking at the drum still in the middle of the room. "You just remember the dark color of your skin and your African heritage is a good thing, a very good thing indeed."